BABY
WANTS
T · H · E
MOON

TO SUSAN PEARSON

Copyright © 1995 by Salvatore Murdocca
All rights reserved. No part of this book may be reproduced or utilized in
any form or by any means, electronic or mechanical, including photo-
copying and recording, or by any information storage and retrieval sys-
tem, without permission in writing from the Publisher. Inquiries should
be addressed to Lothrop, Lee & Shepard Books, a division of William
Morrow & Company, Inc., 1350 Avenue of the Americas, New York, New
York 10019. Printed in Hong Kong.

First Edition   1 2 3 4 5 6 7 8 9 10

Library of Congress Cataloging in Publication Data   Murdocca, Salvatore.
Baby wants the moon / Salvatore Murdocca.   p.   cm. Summary: Sonny
worries about how much his baby sister will grow, especially when she
seems to eat all the time. ISBN 0-688-13664-8. — ISBN 0-688-13665-6
(lib.bdg.)[1. Babies—Fiction. 2. Brothers and sisters—Fiction.]I. Title.
PZ7.M94Bab 1994 [E]—dc20   94-14517 CIP AC

The illustrations in this book were done in watercolor and colored pencil
on Arches paper. The display type was set in Burlington. The text was set in
Garamond. Printed and bound by South China Printing. Production super-
vision by Linda Palladino and Bonnie King. Designed by Robin Ballard.

SALVATORE MURDOCCA

BABY
WANTS
T·H·E
MOON

LOTHROP, LEE & SHEPARD BOOKS   NEW YORK

Sonny watched his mom feed Baby.

"She's always so hungry," he said.

His mother smiled. "Babies need lots of food."

Later he went into Baby's room. He watched her sleep for a long time. Then he tickled her. She started to cry.

"Shhhh," said Sonny.

"What happened?" asked Mom.

"I thought she wanted to play," said Sonny.

"Go out and play with your friends," said his mother. "Baby needs her sleep."

"What's the matter?" asked Phil.

"Why do babies eat and sleep so much?" said Sonny.

"They're busy growing," said Anna. "They grow very fast."

"I don't see her growing," said Sonny.

"They grow at night," said Mike, "when no one is looking."

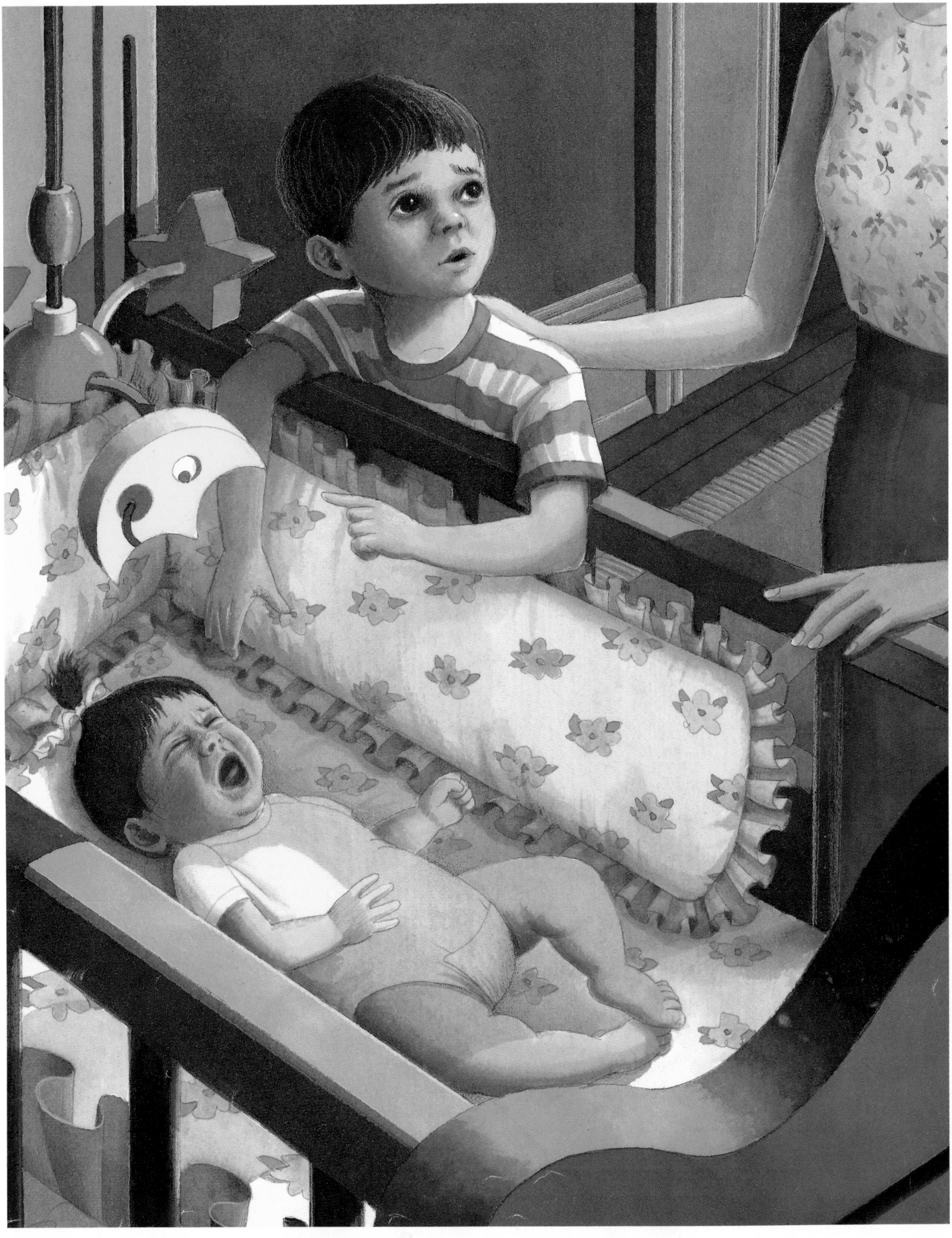

That night Sonny couldn't sleep. He got out of bed and tiptoed down the hall to Baby's room. In the darkness he saw something big in Baby's crib. It was Baby! She filled up the whole crib. Sonny ran back to his room.

In the morning, Baby was small again.
"Baby got really big last night," Sonny told Mom.
"What do you mean?" Mom asked.
"She's growing at night."
"Of course," said Mom. "That's what babies do."
"She's too big for her crib," said Sonny.
Mom smiled. "Not yet," she said.

When Dad came home, he lifted Sonny into the air and kissed him. When he picked up Baby, he groaned and laughed. "My goodness!" he said. "What a big girl! Pretty soon I won't be able to lift you." Baby just gurgled.

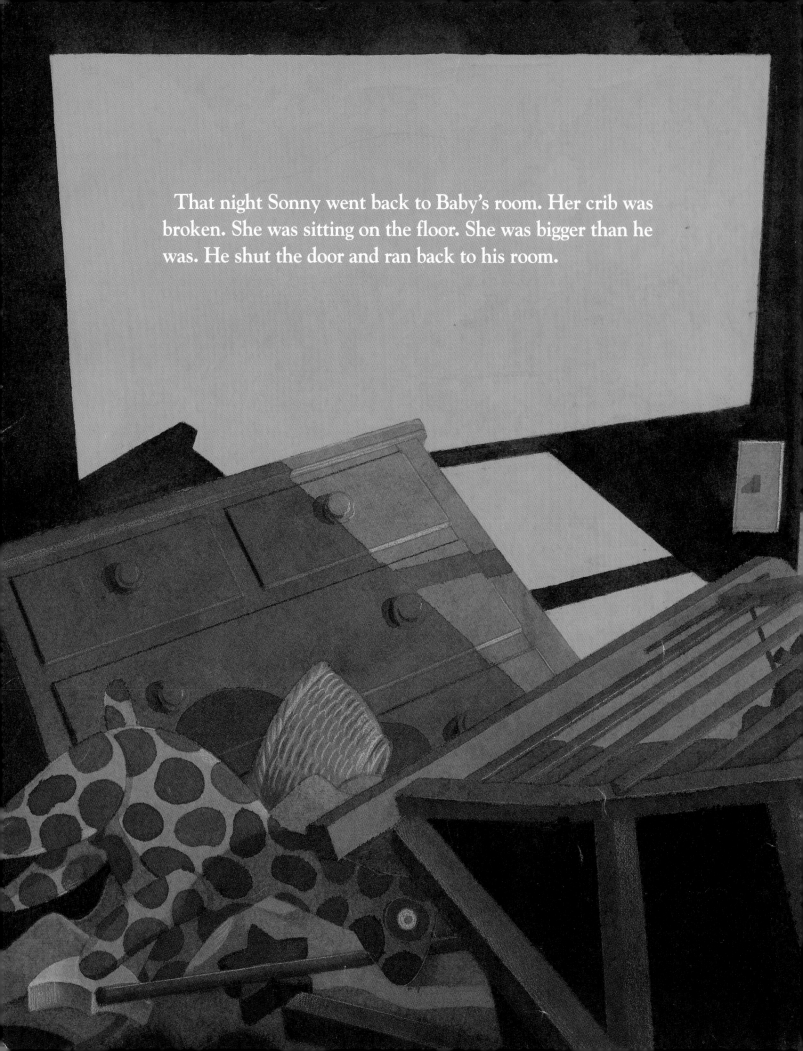

That night Sonny went back to Baby's room. Her crib was broken. She was sitting on the floor. She was bigger than he was. He shut the door and ran back to his room.

In the morning, Baby was small again.

"This baby is growing pretty fast," said Sonny.

"That's right," said Mom.

"Last night she was bigger than me," he said.

"Oh, my," said his mother. "Are you sure?"

"Definitely," said Sonny.

That afternoon Sonny went to Phil's house. Everyone sat in Phil's attic watching Phil's spider.

"I think it's still growing," said Phil.

"So is my baby sister," said Sonny.

"Pretty soon she'll take over the whole house," said Anna.

"Are you sure?" said Sonny.

"Just watch," said Mike. "They eat and eat and eat, and pretty soon the house is too small."

That night Sonny went back to Baby's room. The first thing he saw was Baby's foot. It was almost as big as he was. The rest of the room was filled with Baby. He shut the door carefully and ran back to his room.

Of course, Baby was small again in the morning.

"Mom," said Sonny, "can a baby grow into a giant?"

"Some do," said Mom.

"Baby doesn't fit in her room anymore," said Sonny.

"It is a small room," said Mom, "but I don't think it's serious."

"You don't look so good," said Andy, the delivery boy, as Sonny helped him pick up the groceries. "Is anything wrong?"

"Babies can turn into giants, and my mom doesn't think it's serious," said Sonny.

"Hmmmmm," said Andy, "I see what you mean."

"Do you?" said Sonny.

"Sure I do," said Andy. "I'm in the food business. Every once in a while a kid comes along and eats everybody out of house and home."

"What should I do?" asked Sonny.

"Keep an eye on her," said Andy.

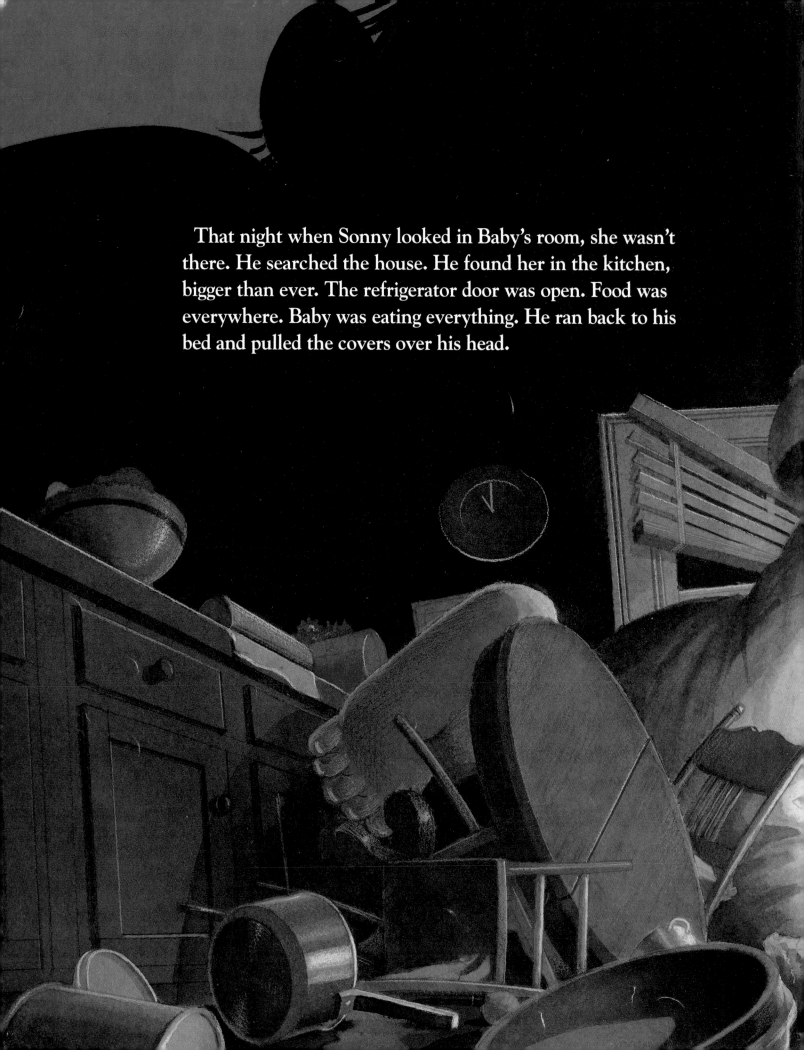

That night when Sonny looked in Baby's room, she wasn't there. He searched the house. He found her in the kitchen, bigger than ever. The refrigerator door was open. Food was everywhere. Baby was eating everything. He ran back to his bed and pulled the covers over his head.

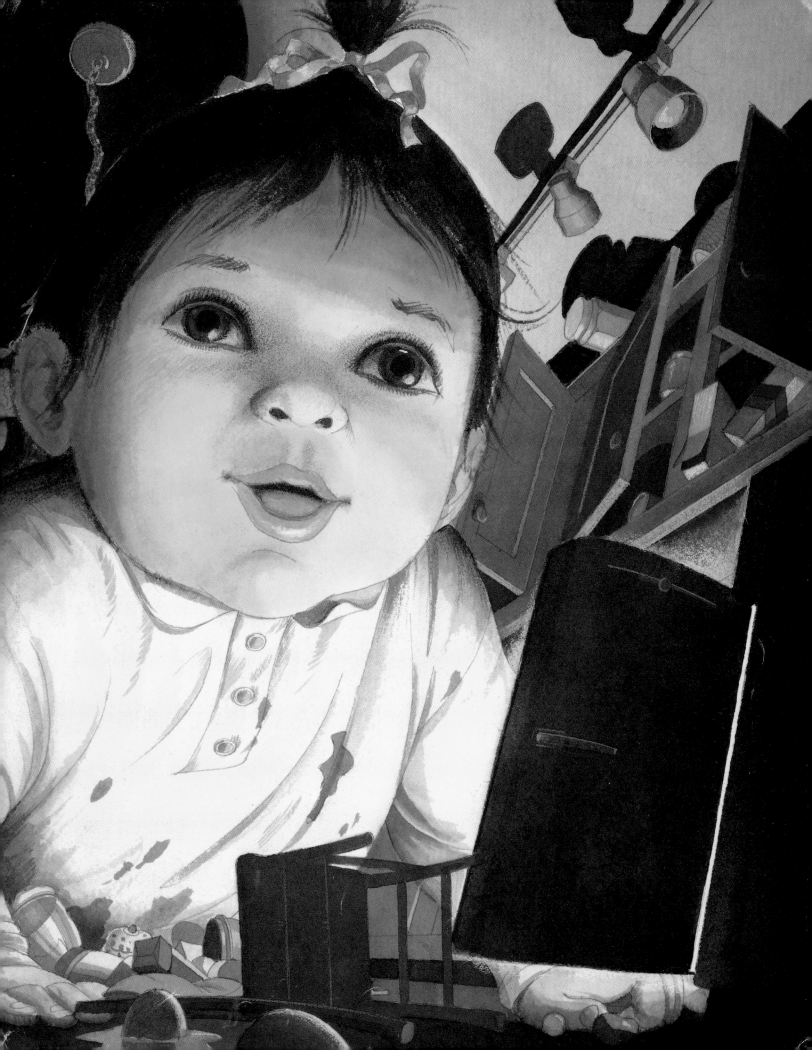

In the morning, the mess was gone and Baby was small again.

"You cleaned up the mess, Mom," said Sonny.

"I always do," said Mom.

"She's going to eat us out of house and home," said Sonny.

Mom looked at Baby and smiled. "Are you going to do that to us?" she teased, and tickled Baby's feet. Baby just laughed.

"When will she stop?" Sonny asked Phil.

Phil thought for a minute. "Not until she has the moon," he said.

"Why would she want the moon?" asked Sonny.

"To eat it," said Phil as he skated down the sidewalk.

"You made that up!" Sonny shouted after him.

"Wait and see," said Phil.

Sonny woke up in the middle of the night and looked out his window. He couldn't believe what he saw. Most of the moon was missing.

He put on his sneakers and went to the back door. He opened it and listened very hard. Above the sound of the crickets, he thought he heard Baby gurgle.

The wet grass smelled sweet. Sonny slipped around to the front of the house. A street lamp lit the empty street. Baby was nowhere to be seen.

Then, from somewhere above, he heard a baby crying. He looked up. There was Baby, bigger than a hot-air balloon.

When she saw Sonny, Baby smiled and pointed at the moon.

Just then Sonny saw something in the moonlight. A long thread, coming all the way from Baby's nightgown, was caught on the fence. He untangled it and tugged. Baby felt lighter than air. He could pull her down with no trouble at all. But when he started to gather in the thread, Baby let out a cry that startled him. The thread slipped through his fingers.

Baby stopped crying. Sonny looked up. She was floating toward the moon, tumbling up and up and up, and laughing.

When Baby reached the moon, she held it like a slice of watermelon. She took a few bites and the moon was gone. But the sky stayed bright from Baby—now *she* was glowing.

But Baby was still hungry. She began to float around the sky, reaching for the stars, but they were too far away. The light inside her began to fade. Baby was disappearing.

Soon the sky was almost black. Sonny could no longer see Baby. Her cry got softer and softer as she reached farther and farther for the stars.

"Baby!" Sonny called. "Don't go away! You'll be small in the morning and Mommy will feed you." But Baby was going away and there was nothing he could do. Sonny started to cry.

When the lamp came on, Mom was sitting on his bed. Baby was asleep in her arms, looking small and soft.

Sonny looked out the window. The moon glowed in the sky.

"You were crying for Baby," said Mom.

Sonny nodded. "Can I please hold her?"

Mom placed Baby in his arms. She opened her eyes and looked at him. Then she gurgled and went back to sleep.

"She's still a pretty small kid," he said.

"But she's growing very fast," said Mom.

"Not THAT fast!" said Sonny.